NURSERY RHYMES

FOR MODERN TIMES

NURSERY RHYMES

FOR MODERN TIMES

XULON PRESS ELITE

ANJO GAMIARHA

Xulon Press
2301 Lucien Way #415
Maitland, FL 32751
407.339.4217
www.xulonpress.com

Printed in the United States of America

Paperback ISBN-13: 978-1-6628-1258-3
Ebook ISBN-13: 978-1-6628-1259-0

Presented to:

From:

Date:

Special Thanks to my illustrators:

HANNAH SEGURA—ILLUSTRATOR OF THE FOLLOWING:
- Cat Lover's Poem
- Dog Lover's Poem
- Molly Le Creep
- Sitting On A Pony
- Some Things Jump
- Dare Devil Dan
- Gabby The Wabby
- Joshua Same
- Silly Sammy Small
- Skateboard Sufer
- If The World Is Round
- Pizza, Burgers, And Fries
- War Is No Fun
- Love Thy Neighbor
*(Note also "Female Rocketship Trip"at the end of the book).

JASON VELAZQUEZ—ILLUSTRATOR OF THE FOLLOWING:
- Wild Animals In The City
- Grandpa Passed My Way
- Betty Plays Ball With The Boys
- Lemonaide Stand
- The Policemen In Our Neighborhood

JEFF EBBLER – ILLUSTRATOR OF THE FOLLOWING:
  -Rocketship Trip *(Note Male on cover of book and poem story illustration in the book)

JEREMY WELLS – ILLUSTRATOR OF THE FOLLOWING:
  -Drippity Droppity Lane

VOX ILLUSTRATION TEAM – ILLUSTRATORS OF THE FOLLOWING:
  -At The End Of The Day We Pray

Introduction

" **N**ursery Rhymes For Modern Times" is a collection of poem stories which will not only inspire today's youth to love literature, but also to love others and the God who made them. Each poem is a unique story unto itself, introducing young readers to new creatures, characters, and creative ways of thinking. Parents, grandparents, and others will enjoy participating by helping the young readers understand how the poems and related bible verses help to reinforce important life principals.

TaBle Of contents

CREATURE RHYMES
- Cat Lover's Poem..5
- Dog Lover's Poem 6
- Molly Le Creep 9
- Sitting on a Pony...10
- Some Things Jump 13
- Wild Animals in the City..14

CHARACTER FINDS
- Dare Devil Dan..17
- Gabby the Wabby...18
- Grandpa Passed My Way 21
- Joshua Same...22
- Silly Sammy Small...25
- Skateboard Sufer 26

CREATIVE TIMES
- Drippity Droppity Lane..29
- If the World Is Round 30
- Pizza, Burgers, and Fries.......................................33
- Rocket Ship Trip 34
- War Is No Fun 37

CHANGING MINDS
- Betty Plays Ball with the Boys..................................38
- Lemonaide Stand...41
- Love My Neighbor 42
- The Policemen in Our Neighborhood...............................45
- At the End of the Day We Pray 46

Cat Lover's Poem

Cats sip tea,
But dogs gnaw on bones.
Cats go exploring,
while dogs run away from home.
Cats wear starched shirts,
but dogs need collars.
Cats are always polite,
dog's always holler.
Cats attend school,
while dogs run the streets.
Cats are very tidy,
but dogs are never neat.
Cats hunt mice,
and dogs chase cars.
Cat's belong to country clubs,
while dogs hang out in bars.
Cats are quite civilized,
but dogs must be tamed.
Cats are born intelligent.
But dogs? They need a cat's brain!

Genesis 1:25-"God made the beasts of the earth after their kind, and the cattle after their kind, and everything that creeps on the ground after its kind; and God saw that it was good."

Dog Lover's Poem

Dogs are like friends,
cats are like fiends.
Dogs are very loyal,
but cats split the scene.
Dogs love to protect you,
While cats are just for show.
Dogs are obedient,
but cats just say "no."
Dogs work real hard,
as cats just lay down.
Dogs run in packs,
but cats don't want you around.
Dogs give their all,
while cats play it cool.
Dogs are appreciative.
But cats? They need to attend dog school!

Proverbs 12:10A–"A righteous man has regard for the life of his animal."

Molly Le Creep

There's a girl down the street named Molly Le Creep. She collects
all kinds of things alive. She has guppies and puppies, kittens and cats.
She has chickens and pigeons, and even some rats. And if you look real close beside her,
you'll even see her pet spider!

She has a snake and a lizard, both named Wizard. She has a goose, some
snails, and a duck. She has seed-eating parrots, and rabbits that eat carrots, and even
some weird thing that's called a ferret.

Molly has a frog named Hog and of course a guinea pig. She knows all about the places
her animals live. In fact, she can tell you everything about them you'd ever want to know,
(and even some things you dont' wanna). But it's best to listen to Molly Le Creep when she's
holding her giant iguana!

What a squirrel of a girl, that Molly Le Creep, to love all those things that fly, crawl, and
squeak. Evern her mom says, "Molly is different, it's true. She's not like me and you. And
it just might be her place, in his human race, to grow up and manage a zoo!"

Genesis 7:1-3-"Then the Lord said to Noah, enter the ark, you and all your household, for you alone I
have seen to righteous before me in this time. You shall take with you of every clean animal by sevens,
a male and his female; and of the animals that are not clean two,a male and his female; also of the
birds of the sky, by sevens, male and female, to keep offspring alive on the face of the earth."

Sitting On A Pony

Sitting on a pony,
I'm feeling really dumb.

I've got my hat on my head,
and hand on my gun.

Grandpa's just smiling,
Daddy's having fun.

Camera man is ready,
So I say, "hurry get this done!"

John 12:14-15 – "Jesus, finding a young donkey, sat on it; as it is written, Fear not daughter of Zion, behold, your King is coming, seated on a donkey's colt."

Some Things Jump!

Some things jump,

and some things don't.

Grasshoppers can,

but hippos won't.

Frogs they will,

but elephants don't.

Rabbits they do,

but rhinos won't.

Kangarees can,

But king crabs don't.

Cause some things jump,

and some things don't!

Genesis 7:13-14–"On the very same day Noah and Shem and Ham and Japheth, the sons of Noah, and Noah's wife and the three wives of his sons with them, entered the ark, they and every beast after it's kind, and all the cattle after their kind, and every creeping thing that creeps on the earth after its kind, and every bird after its kind, all sorts of birds."

Wild Animals In The City

Racoon in the trash can,

I thought it was a cat.

Opossum in the bushes,

they looked a lot like rats.

I heard birds in the attic,

but mom said it might be bats.

Wild animals in the city,

who would imagine that?

Isaiah 11:6–"And the wolf will dwell with the lamb, and the leopard will lie down with the young goat, and the calf and the young lion and the fatling together; and a little boy shall lead them."

Daredevil Dan

Daredevil Dan,

was dangerous on a bike.

Jumped over his sister Nan,

and landed on his brother Mike.

He broke his collar bone,

but his brother was o.k.

And everyone knew,

Dan would end up that way!

Matthew 14:28-30–"Peter said to Him, Lord if it is you, command me to come to you on the water. And He said, 'Come!' And Peter got out of the boat, and walked on the water and came toward Jesus. But seeing the wind he became frightened and beginning to sink he cried out 'Lord save me!'"

Gabby The Wabby

There is a girl name Gabby,

but people call her Wabby.

People call her Wabby,

cause she wiggles all the time.

She wiggles when she wakes,

and she wiggles when she walks.

She wiggles when she wants.

She just wiggles rain or shine.

She wiggles when at school.

She's a real wiggly fool.

To her it's oh so cool,

but it blows her teacher's mind.

Psalms 139:14–"I give thanks to You, for I am fearfully and wonderfully made; wonderful are your works and my soul knows it very well."

My Grandpa Passed My Way

They say today,
my Grandpa passed away,
and it would be awhile,
before I'd see him again.

But I remember everything,
he used to say,
and all the time he spent,
just being my friend.

My mother said,
I can hold on to memories of him,
but really they hold on to me.
Cause even though I can't see his face,
I still feel his love all over me.

My father said,
Grandpa's in a better place,
but I can't imagine where that place would be.
All I know is it will be better,
when I meet up with him again,
and again my best friend will be with me.

John 11:25-"Jesus said to her, I am the resurrection and the life he who believes in me will live even if he dies."

Joshua Same

There is a boy named Joshua Same,

who has a particular claim to fame.

He is known as the best,

must better than the rest,

at playing video games.

Sometimes he plays all day,

Prompting his mother to say,

"Oh Josh it's a shame,

to waste your good brain,

in such a frivolous way."

Proverbs 20:11-"It is by his deeds that a lad distinguishes himself if his conduct is pure and right."

Silly Sammy Small

Silly Sammy Small, is a boy who loves to play with his soccer ball.

He kicks it to school and takes it to class.

When it's time for lunch he dribbles it fast.

Even when walking in the school hall,

Sammy does headers off the wall with his ball.

And I think that breaks some rule I recall.

But Silly Sammy Small, would never give up his soccer ball!

I Samuel 17:42-46–"When the Philistine looked and saw David, he disdained him; for he was but a youth, and ruddy, with a handsome appearance....Then David said to the Philistine, You come to me with a sword, a spear, and a javelin, but I come to you in the name of the Lord of hosts....This day the Lord will deliver you up into my hands..."

Skateboard Surfer

I'm a cement surfer.

A real cool turfer.

Some dudes see a driveway,

but I see a real hard wave.

When I come to the pavement end,

I like to hang ten.

And when I jump a ramp I shout,

"look out below wipe out!"

Proverbs 27:12–"A prudent man sees evil and hides himself, The naive proceed and pay the penalty."

Drippity Droppity Lane

Drippity Droppity Lane,
is a place where it always rains.
The creatures there dress insane,
some in top hats, some in coats and canes.

There are Gaint snells in neon shells,
that brighten up the slippery trails.
Helping everyone to see,
what goes on in Drippity Droppity.

There are also flying fish,
that meet in midair with a kiss.
Plaid platypuses on rollers,
purple pandas pushing babes in strollers.

But what makes Droppity so neat,
is that the creatures there are at peace,
cause the rain makes everyone sweet,
in Drippity Droppity Lane!

Revelation 21:4-"and He will wipe away every tear from their eyes: and there will no longer be any death; and there will no longer be any mouring, or crying, or pain; the first things have passed away."

If The World Is Round

If the world is round,

and is spinning round and round,

and is going round the sun on it's way.

Then when I'm standing on the ground,

as the world goes round and round,

then why don't I get dizzy everyday?

Tell me that!

Why don't I get dizzy everyday?

Isaiah 40:22: "It is He who sits above the circle of the earth, and it's inhabitants are like grasshoppers, Who stretches out the heavens like a curtains and spreads them out like a tent to dwell in."

Pizza, Burgers, And Fries

Pizza, Burgers, and Fries,

decided to leave town.

Then all the children cried,

so they stopped and turned around.

Pizza said, "we'll stay."

Burgers said, "o.k."

Then Fries replied, "but you all must decide,

to eat your veggies everyday."

I Timothy 4:4–"For everything created by God is good, and nothing is to be rejected, if it is received with gratitude; for it is sanctified by means of the word of God and prayer."

Rocket Ship Trip

If I could take a trip,

on a rocket ship,

I'd ride it like a horsey,

I'd lasso all the stars.

I'd visit all the planets,

Uranus, Pluto, Mars.

I'd camp out on the moon,

space songs I would croon.

Then I'd go exploring,

in black holes just for fun,

and if that got too boring,

I'd ride off towards the sun.

Genesis 1:16-"God made the two great lights, the greater light to govern the day, and the lesser light to govern the night; He made the stars also."

War Is No Fun

It's fun to play soldiers,

with all of my friends;

cause when the game is over,

no one is hurt at the end.

We use our imagination,

and of course our toy guns,

and if we get shot,

we can still run.

Real war is not like that.

My dad has been in some.

He says there's no laughter.

Cause real war is no fun!

Isaiah 2:4–"And He will judge between the nations, and will render decisions for many peoples....Nation wil not lift up sword against nation, and never again wil they learn war."

Betty Plays Ball With The Boys

Betty plays ball with the boys,

and some of them don't like it.

But they really don't have a choice,

because she made the team inspite of it.

Her dad taught her to pitch,

when she was only a tike at it.

Now it's hard to hit,

her curve ball or even catch sight of it.

Her pony tails are all they see,

as she winds up to let go of it.

They strike out one-two- three,

and that makes her dad crow a bit!

Galatians 3:28–"There is neither Jew nor Greek, there is neither slave nor free man, there is neither male nor female; for you are all one in Christ Jesus."

Lemonaide Stand

One day we saw a man,

standing by our lemonaide stand.

He looked so all alone.

Mom said he had no home.

So, we came up with a plan,

to help the homeless man.

We used our profits alone,

to help him get a home!

Luke 10:30-37–"Jesus replied and said, a man was going down from Jerusalem to Jericho, and fell among robbers, and they stripped him and beat him, and went away leaving him half dead. And by chance a priest was going down on that road, and when he saw him he passed by on the other side. Likewise a Levite also, when he came to the place and saw him, passed by on the other side. But a Samaritan, who was on a journey, came upon him; and when he saw him he felt compassion….and he brought him to an inn and took care of him….Which of these three do you think proved to be a neighbor to the man who fell into the robbers hands? And he said, the one who showed mercy for him. Then Jesus said to him, go and do the same."

Love My Neighbor

A lot of people live on my block,
some I don't even know.
Some wave hi as they walk by,
others look away as they go.

Different people live on my block,
they come from all over the world.
There is an old man from Japan,
a young boy from Hanoi,
and even an Indian girl.

I like the people who live on my block,
They have interesting stories to tell,
about where they come from,
and how they have fun,
and what makes their food smell so swell.

I can't understand some of the people on my block,
they talk different and keep to themselves.
But I remember the rule,
I learned in Sunday School,
to love my neighbor as myself.

Matthew 22:36-39–"Teacher, which is the great commandment in the Law? And He said to him, You shall love the Lord your God with all your heart, and with all your soul, and with all your mind....The second is like it, You shall love your neighbor as yourself."

The Policemen In My Neighborhood

Late at night, when everyone is asleep,
It's dark outside and quiet on the streets.
A black and white car slowly creeps,
around my neighborhood.

It's the policemen, alert and strong,
making sure no one is in harm.
They check for any sudden alarm,
in my neighborhood.

Their jobs are hard, and they can make mistakes.
Sometimes when called the bad guyes escape.
But having them around makes folks feel safe,
in my neighborhood.

Romans 13:3-4-"For rulers are not a cause of fear for good behavior, but for evil. Do you want to have no fearof authority? Do what is good and you will have praise from the same; for it is a minister of God to you for good."

At The End Of The Day We Pray

At the end of the day that the Lord has made,

my family and I bow our heads to pray.

We thank him for his blessings,

both big and small.

We thank him that he loves us most of all.

We ask him for forgiveness,

for any bad things we have done.

And to forgive those,

who have done us wrong.

Then we end our prayers,

in a very simple way,

that his will would be done,

each and every day.

Matthew 6:9-13–"Pray then, in this way: Our Father who is in heaven, Hallowed be Your name. Your kingdom come. Your will be done, on earth as it isin heaven. Give us this day our daily bread. And forgive us our debts, as we also have forgiven our debtors. And do not lead us into temptation, but deliver us from evil. For yours is the kingdom, and the power, and the glory forever. Amen."

All things are possible to him who believes.- Mark 9:23